Anonymous

Services at the Funeral of Martha

Wife of Hovey K. Clarke

Anonymous

Services at the Funeral of Martha
Wife of Hovey K. Clarke

ISBN/EAN: 9783337715199

Printed in Europe, USA, Canada, Australia, Japan

Cover: Foto ©Raphael Reischuk / pixelio.de

More available books at **www.hansebooks.com**

DETROIT, JUNE 3, 1869.

SERVICES

AT THE

FUNERAL OF MARTHA,

WIFE OF HOVEY K. CLARKE,

DAUGHTER OF TIMOTHY AND ELIZA (ADAMS) UPHAM.

CONDUCTED BY THE REV. W. E. McLAREN, PASTOR OF WESTMINSTER
CHURCH; AND THE REV. GEORGE WORTHINGTON, RECTOR
OF ST. JOHN'S CHURCH, DETROIT.

Printed for Private Circulation.

THE SERVICES

Were commenced at the late residence of the deceased, by reading : —

MAN that is born of a woman is of few days, and full of trouble. He cometh forth like a flower, and is cut down: he fleeth also as a shadow, and continueth not. — JOB xiv. 1, 2.

All flesh is grass, and all the goodliness thereof is as the flower of the field. — ISA. xl. 6.

In the morning they are like grass which groweth up. In the morning it flourisheth, and groweth up; in the evening it is cut down and withereth. — PS. xc. 5, 6.

If a man die, shall he live again? —JOB xiv. 14.

Jesus said unto her, I am the resurrection and the life: he that believeth in me, though he were dead, yet shall he live; and whosoever liveth and believeth in me, shall never die. Believest thou this? —JOHN xi. 25, 26.

But now is Christ risen from the dead, and become the first-fruits of them that slept. For since by man came death, by man came also the resurrection of the dead. For as in Adam all die, even so in Christ shall all be made alive. But every man in his own order: Christ the first-fruits; afterward they that are Christ's at his coming. Then cometh the end, when he shall have delivered up the kingdom to God, even the Father; when he shall have put down all rule, and all authority and power. For he must reign, till he hath put all enemies under his feet. The last enemy that shall be destroyed is death. — 1 COR. xv. 20–26.

But some man will say, How are the dead raised up? and with what body do they come?

Thou fool, that which thou sowest is not quickened, except it die; and that which thou sowest, thou sowest not that body that shall be, but bare grain; it may chance of wheat, or of some other grain: but God giveth it a body

as it hath pleased him, and to every seed his own body. —
1 COR. XV. 35–38.

So also is the resurrection of the dead. It is sown in
corruption; it is raised in incorruption: it is sown in dis-
honor; it is raised in glory: it is sown in weakness; it is
raised in power: it is sown a natural body; it is raised
a spiritual body. There is a natural body, and there is a
spiritual body. — 1 COR. XV. 42–44.

Now this I say, brethren, that flesh and blood cannot
inherit the kingdom of God; neither doth corruption
inherit incorruption.

Behold, I show you a mystery; we shall not all sleep,
but we shall all be changed, in a moment, in the twinkling
of an eye, at the last trump: for the trumpet shall sound,
and the dead shall be raised incorruptible, and we shall be
changed. For this corruptible must put on incorruption,
and this mortal must put on immortality. So when this
corruptible shall have put on incorruption, and this mortal shall have put on immortality, then shall be brought to
pass the saying that is written, Death is swallowed up in
victory.

O Death, where is thy sting? O Grave, where is thy
victory?

The sting of death is sin ; and the strength of sin is the law. But thanks be to God, which giveth us the victory through our Lord Jesus Christ. — 1 COR. XV. 50-57.

—◆—

Prayer.

—◆—

WHY do we mourn departing friends,
    Or shake at death's alarms ?
'T is but the voice that Jesus sends,
    To call them to his arms.

Why should we tremble to convey
    Their bodies to the tomb ?
There the dear flesh of Jesus lay,
    And left a long perfume.

The graves of all the saints he blest,
    And softened every bed ;
Where should the dying members rest,
    But with their dying Head?

ADDRESS

By the Rev. William E. McLaren,

Pastor of Westminster Church, Detroit.

A WISE man of old has said that there is a time to
weep, and a time to rejoice. Accustomed as we
are to regard the emotions of grief and joy as distinct
and opposite, it seems, at first sight, quite paradoxical to
declare that they are not, necessarily, antagonistic. But
we have only to analyze the feelings which we experience at this moment, as we stand around the bier of
this beloved saint of God, to be convinced that there
are times when sorrow and gladness are not, necessarily,
inconsistent with each other, — when grief may sanctify
joy with her tears, and joy illumine and glorify grief
with her smiles.

When we look upon this inanimate form, and mark how the light of love has for ever faded from this beautiful face, we say, This is death! And yet it is only seeming death.

Fortified by the teachings of the Holy Word, pointing to the triumphant illustration of those teachings in the character and experience of this departed saint, we are bold to oppose the appearance with the reality, and deny to Death the right of conqueror here. These burial rites are not his triumphal procession. Yonder waiting grave is not the gate of his prison-house. On the contrary, we celebrate to-day the death of Death, and, with exultation, cry, " O Death, where is thy sting ? O Grave, where is thy victory ? "

True, there is loss here; but I repeat it, this is not death. It would be idle to ignore the wounds of stricken Nature. Bitter, indeed, is the cup of bereavement. Dark, dark, are those Gethsemanes of grief, into whose gloom and agony we must needs enter. Who can stop the flow of tears, or stifle the heaving sigh, when the tendrils of affection are torn from the objects around which they had entwined themselves? The bereft spirit *will* shrink and tremble when those whom we love are taken from us, and we are assured that we shall see their faces here no more for ever. It is Nature's right. That perfect Human Life, which Heaven gave the world for its shining model, was not too pure, too lofty, for tears. For Him who loved Martha and her sister and Lazarus, there was a time to weep; and when he stood at the grave, troubled in spirit, we are told that "Jesus wept."

But the same blessed Lord, who justifies our grief, has also illustrated the consistency of triumph and joy with the bitterness of bereavement. As at the funeral of the widow's son, at Nain, he says now, "Weep not!" Weep not, for in his love — his love for us, which was unto death (which loving death gave us eternal life) — is to be found the antidote of tears. Nature *must* weep; but oh, Faith will paint rainbows on those tears! Nature looks downward upon the calamity; but Faith eyes the victory yonder. Nature cannot forget the long weeks of suffering; but Faith melts to rapture with thinking of the joy of the spirit that is home at last. Nature staggers at the coming loneliness and separation; but Faith leans calmly on God, and knows that the voice which once sang —

> " For thee, O dear, dear Country,
>   Mine eyes their vigils keep ;
> For very love, beholding
>   Thy happy name, they weep,"

is now joining in the praise of the Redeemer, and cele-
brating the honor of Him by whom there is salvation
from the sins and the sorrows of life.

With reference to the beautiful life which made this
home radiant with Christian virtue and purity, I can say
nothing but what is already known to you. Her character was transparent. She was a child of the light and
of day. The virtues that are perpetuated on marble
often begin there, but our eulogies to-day shall be simply the expression of the common sentiment of all;
for —

> " None knew her but to love her :
>   None named her but to praise."

The first impression which her character makes upon
the mind is that of completeness. There was a round-
ness and symmetry in it which the world too seldom
sees. Completeness is not perfection. The holiest
saint this side of heaven has the scars of past, and the
bleeding wounds of present, sins. " If we say that we

have no sin, we deceive ourselves, and the truth is not in us." But the life of faith in the Son of God implies a progressive dying unto sin and living unto righteousness, — a gradual assimilation of the whole nature to the ideal humanity of Christ. This process tends to unify all the qualities of the soul. Subordinated all to the Divine Will, they grow each like the other, and combine in beautiful harmony. There was this peculiar finish of Christian character in Mrs. Clarke. Unsanctified traits did not protrude at times, and mar the beauties of her life. She was uniformly the calm, earnest, persistent follower of her Lord. If she never soared to enthusiasm as high as some, she never experienced as serious depressions. The type of her piety was more like that of John than of Peter, of Mary than of Martha.

Her religion was pervasive of her whole life; and hence, we cannot, without doing violence to its completeness, regard her spiritual character separately from her character as manifested in social and domestic life. She was *one*. She was everywhere, and in all relations, Christian. From earliest life, she was the joy and delight of a New-England home. For it, she was a beaming sun in the beauty of the day, — a guiding star

in the darkness of the night, — always shining for others. In the dewy freshness of maidenhood, she was
called to take up the cross of physical suffering, and at
once made affliction beautiful by her meek and quiet
acquiescence in God's will. For seventeen years, she
has adorned and sanctified the married state with the
devotion of a heart in which there were wonderful
capacities of affection. Gifted beyond the usual lot of
woman, with a mingled dignity and sweetness of presence, which exercised a charm almost magnetic upon
others; possessed of mental qualities whose powers
were polished and beautified by culture, with a poetic
taste for the true, the beautiful, and the good, she was
predestined to shine in the social circle; and she re-
ceived, all through her life, with a courtly grace, the
homage of a large company of admiring friends, and yet
with such unconsciousness of herself, that only they
knew how queenly she was.

With so pronounced spirituality of heart, also, she
could not choose but render her capabilities tributary
to the cause of her Lord Jesus Christ. As a member
of his Holy Church, she was faithful, devoted, practi-
cal. With a surpassingly beautiful catholic spirit, she

loved all who love our Lord in sincerity and truth; and when physical infirmity conspired with conjugal affection to lead her reverent spirit to another than the altar of her youthful choice and conviction, she became an interested participant in every work and labor of love there, and sweetly identified herself with what she felt to be a due worship of the Father Almighty, and a proper and profitable sacramental contact with the adorable Christ; so that, to-day, around her silent form, it is the grateful privilege of two separate Christian communions to mingle their tears and unite their last offices to the dead.

In all these relations, it seems to me, I can discern that remarkable completeness, that finish and symmetry of character, of which I have spoken.

But you will agree with me, that the peculiar beauty of the character over whose departure we weep, and over whose elevation to the skies we rejoice, to-day, consisted in the meek and cheerful spirit with which she accepted suffering. Peculiarly afflicted through a long series of years, she was also peculiarly strengthened to endure. In her, patience had its perfect work.

Why, you may ask, should *she* have suffered so severely? Why should a pure and gentle being like her be selected to bear the heaviest burden of pain? Surely, it could not be that she deserved to suffer more than many less lovely beings who also suffer less. It is never wise to interpret Providence by appearances. The book of God's eternal purposes is a closed book. It will not be opened, neither will we be capable of reading it, until the day when we shall give our account before the judgment-seat of Christ. It is often impossible to explain the dealings of God with us. They are inscrutable. Why the good should suffer, and the wicked go free, is a mystery, at which we often stumble. But surely all is clear, in this instance. Is it not plain to all, that Mrs. Clarke's life-work was to exemplify the power of the Christian faith in suffering? Can we not look back now, and see that it was for this God sent her into the world; for this he gave her a long life of pain, culminating, at last, in trials of peculiar aggravation, that he might teach men how, by the operation of the Christian philosophy, we may be made perfect through suffering? Above nearly all of the dear fellow-sufferers of Christ whom I have known.

she was enabled to exemplify the patience of the gospel, the patience which is not stoicism, shutting its eyes to suffering and blunting the soul's sensibilities that it may not feel a pang; not a dumb, fatalistic fainting under affliction, but cheerful resignation, courageous acceptance of the inevitable, because a wise God has made it so. This is the spirit which says, —

> " He kindles for my profit purely
> Affliction's glowing, fiery brand,
> And all his heaviest blows are surely
> Inflicted by a loving hand ;
> So I say gladly, ' *As God will,*'
> And trust in him, and suffer still."

This was the noblest lesson of this departed life, — to show how, by faith, the disciple of Christ may turn and kiss the hand that wields the rod, and so grow purer and more heavenly-minded for the smiting.

The fruit of this experience, reached neither you nor I can tell by what agonies of body and mind, was the development, in her, of that shining quality of self-forgetfulness, which is the choicest grace the Spirit can bestow upon a believer. By the process of discipline, she had become transformed into the likeness of Christ;

and so, by a sweet spontaneity, her gentle heart was ever plotting some deed of love, or kindly word. She was never so happy as when making others happy. It was real joy to her to minister to others, and yet she was all unconscious that many looked upon her with wonder; and beholding her thoughtfulness of others, when suffering seemed to give her a sacred right to think only of self, loved to fancy at times that she was one of those holier natures whom God sends into this world on embassies of love to serve Salvation's heirs.

This, I say, was eminently her mission, to illustrate Christian faith in suffering, in her subjective qualities of soul, and as well in her active relations to those around her; and there are many, very many, here and elsewhere, who will rise up and call her blessed, in return for the benedictions she has often unconsciously shed on them, and the holy lessons she has taught them.

It was a sore trial to faith that the promise should seem to fail of literal fulfilment, that "at the evening time it shall be light;" but it was a fit finale to all, that the last testimony of consciousness should reveal the spirit still leaning in the accustomed attitude of faith on the will of Him who doeth all things well.

I have seen a golden sun rise and climb to the merid-
ian in great glory; and then, as evening crept apace, I
have seen his radiant face enveloped in clouds and darkness, and his setting seemed to be a thing of terror, —
black with storm, lurid with the red leaps of electric
arrows, — and all the world has trembled. But do I
forget that the clouds are only local, and that the tem-
pest is but for an hour? and do I forget, that, behind
the terrors of the western sky, the bright sun rolls on
as calmly, as steadily, as goldenly, as he did in the
morning?

Thus, behind the physical distress which rendered the
closing of this life so trying, who can, for a moment,
doubt that the beautiful Christian soul was moving
peacefully on, and that, even in the Valley of the Shadow
of Death, she feared no evil? Who can doubt, that,
while "the swellings of Jordan" rolled madly about
her, the soul's eye was gazing, with transports of expec-
tation, upon "the fair and happy land" beyond? Yes,
loved saint, we know that the darkness and the storm
were soon passed, and then —

" The sunshine of heaven beamed bright on thy waking,
  And the song that thou heard'st was the seraphims' song."

She died as God would have her die; and the unearthly beauty of that vanishing face seems to speak to us of the spotless holiness of the disembodied spirit which shines now and evermore among the multitudes of the blessed.

And now we are to lay her body gently down to sleep. She did not wish to survive the coming of the summer, and so her heavenly-Father called his child home on June's first day, — a day of beauty and brightness, — a day, too, to her of festal memories of other years. With a sacred sorrow and a chastened joy, we can ask room for her dear dust upon the bosom of its mother Earth; and we can ask these flowers she so much loved to go with her, and we can bid others take their station over her sleeping form, and keep ceaseless vigil there.

But, best of all, we can commit this body to the grave, in the assured belief that the very dust of his people is dear to God, and that it is true which Jesus said to Martha: —

"I am the resurrection and the life: he that believeth in me, though he were dead, yet shall he live. And whosoever liveth and believeth in me, shall never die."

JESUS, the very thought of thee
   With gladness fills my breast;
But dearer far thy face to see,
   And in thy presence rest.

Nor voice can sing, nor heart can frame,
   Nor can the memory find,
A sweeter sound than thy blest name,
   O Saviour of mankind!

O Hope of every contrite heart!
   O Joy of all the meek!
To those who fall, how kind thou art!
   How good to those who seek!

And those who find thee, find a bliss
   Nor tongue nor pen can show:
The love of Jesus, — what it is
   None but his loved ones know.

THE remains of the "blessed dead" were now taken from the house, to be borne to Elmwood Cemetery, in the charge of General W. F. RAYNOLDS, Mr. LEWIS ALLEN, Mr. D. BETHUNE DUFFIELD, Mr. JAMES A. ARMSTRONG, Mr. H. P. BALDWIN, Mr. ALFRED RUSSELL, Mr. JOHN G. ERWIN, and Mr. E. WILLARD SMITH.

At Elmwood, the burial service of the Episcopal Church was read by the Rev. GEORGE WORTHINGTON, Rector of St. John's, Detroit.

A^ND NOW, — although the solemn cadence of the
service, "earth to earth, ashes to ashes, dust to
dust," has fallen, yet the impulses of affection still plead
for expression.

Flowers, which had bloomed nearly a thousand miles
apart, the offerings of dear friends thus widely separated,
here met, and were wrought into expressive forms, —
the cross, the wreath, the crown, the star; symboliz-
ing the trials, the triumphs, and the rewards of one who,
through faith and patience, has inherited the promises.
The sod which was broken that the earth might

> "Take this new treasure to its trust,"

is replaced; and the Cross, the Wreath, and the Crown
mark the spot beneath which reposes the dust of the precious dead; and all that respect and affection can do
is done.

THE CROSS! She had borne the cross, — the cross of physical suffering in her youth. She had carried it through the years of her mature life; and that so patiently and so cheerfully, as scarcely to exhibit the consciousness of it to her nearest and dearest friends. But not in her own strength. She early knew, and had grown from day to day and from year to year more strong in the knowledge of the strength derived from union with the Divine Sufferer, who suffered on the cross of Calvary. And, at the last, when speech had failed her, her right arm paralyzed, with the left she could still express her unfaltering trust in the cross by pointing to the symbol hanging in her sight, and, with a trustful gesture, to the illuminated words, " Simply to thy cross I cling."

THE WREATH. Patience under physical suffering, habitual and often severe, had wrought in her its perfect work; and the victory of her spirit, over the various forms in which it assailed her throughout the years of her invalid life, was complete. At the close, a new and severe test awaited her. A gradual paralysis of the organs of speech, at first permitting her to speak only with difficulty, then more and more imperfectly, at last closed this avenue of her thoughts and desires completely. Perhaps it would be an impulse of Christian emotion, which, desiring to express, she would labor patiently, and sometimes painfully, until, as in one instance, it was perceived that her thought was in the New Testament, — in the Acts, — in the fourth chapter; and then that it was the last words of the dying Stephen, dwelling devoutly in her heart, that she desired to utter, — "Lord Jesus, receive my spirit." Or, perhaps, it was some direction for the comfort of her family, — some message or gift, as a parting word or memento of affection; and her face would glow with satisfaction, when, at last, she was enabled to render her thought clear; but, when she failed to make herself understood, her sad moan of disappointment was a most touching proof of the severity of this new trial, that so darkly shrouded the last days of her life. Can it be the exaggeration of an overwrought affection which discerns, in the patience with which these trials were borne, a victor worthy of the conqueror's wreath?

THE CROWN. The crown is sure; for, of such suffering and such faith, it was written, " If so be that we

suffer with him, that we may be also glorified together "
(Rom. viii. 17); "If we suffer, we shall also reign with
him " (2 Tim. ii. 12); "Henceforth there is laid up for
me a crown of righteousness, which the Lord, the
righteous Judge, shall give me at that day " (2 Tim.
iv. 8).

THE STAR. The example of such a life is a precious
memory. Its effulgent beams invite and point the way
to follow. Its sweet influences for good will always be
gratefully remembered by many who have felt its power.
Its reward is the reward of those who turn many to
righteousness; and, in all the sorrow of bereavement,
there may be thankful rejoicings that she shall shine as
a STAR for ever and ever.

These symbols, in their beautiful but ephemeral forms,
will fade. So will the flowers which decked the bed on
which the body of the lovely sleeper was laid for the
rest of the grave. But the memories they symbolize
will bloom with perpetual verdure. And so will the
love which prompted these graceful offerings, and that
of those who sought, with watchful solicitude, to soothe

the last days of the departed, be ever cherished by those whose right and duty it is to be grateful for such services. But more, and higher and better still, He who, with the affection of an Elder Brother at once human and divine, regarded the love bestowed upon his loved one, will say, " Inasmuch as ye did it unto her, ye did it unto me."

Tributes.

Contributed to the Detroit "Daily Advertiser and Tribune" of Thursday evening, June 3d : —

DEPARTED this life, Tuesday morning, June 1, 1869, MARTHA U., wife of Hovey K. Clarke, and daughter of the late General Timothy Upham, of Portsmouth, N.H.

The large circle of friends, to which this announcement brings inexpressible sorrow, will be comforted by some expression of the thoughts which must come to them all, as they mourn over the vacant place, and lovingly recall the pleasant memories of a companionship so unfailingly brightening and helpful and true; and yet words can do but little to convey the charm of a life which they all *felt* as a *power*, and knew to be one of the good gifts from above. But now that the humility with which she was clothed cannot be wounded, we may feel that her attainment in the Christian life is our treasure, — a "living epistle," which we may strive to read, with the hope to catch something of its spirit.

To the friends of her married life, who have only
known her as an invalid, the patience with which she
bore her sufferings, and the cheerful courage with which
she resisted the depressing effect of almost constant
physical pain, have been evidences of a strength which
could only come from one source, — the grace which
she ever so trustingly sought, and whose sanctifying influences were daily forming in her the likeness to the
dear Lord, whose gift of love she knew her cross to be.
If she felt the burden, none knew it. Those who saw
her meeting the daily duties of life, in her family and
socially, could scarcely suspect its existence; and her
genuine enjoyment of her home and friends was all the
deeper, perhaps, because of the constant victory over
physical infirmity with which it was purchased; so that,
when, a year ago, greatly increased suffering told her
that her pilgrimage was drawing to an end, it called
her to just as poignant a sundering of the earthly ties as
when the summons comes to one in full health; and
earth with all its natural beauty was lovely, and her
friends dear and ever in her thoughts, to the last con-
scious hour of her life. As each month, and finally
each week, brought its added weight of pain, with

it came the fulfilment of the promises in which she trusted, and the "fiery trial" never seemed "some strange thing" to her, who could rejoice, inasmuch as she was a partaker of Christ's sufferings. She could ever meekly say, —

"O Lord my God, do thou thy holy will,
      I will lie still :
I will not stir, lest I forsake thine arm,
      And break the charm,
Which lulls me, clinging to my Father's breast,
      In perfect rest ! "

Beyond the home circle, whose light she was, many hearts are aching with a sense of personal loss, and own her quiet influence for good, — so quiet, that, perhaps, only in the losing of it will its true value be known. May they all be lifted up to follow her in thought to the blessed rest of paradise, and to give thanks for the grace through which she triumphed: "having the testimony of a good conscience; in the communion of the Catholic Church; in the confidence of a certain faith; in the comfort of a reasonable, religious, and holy hope; in favor with God; and in perfect charity with the world."

DETROIT, June 3, 1869.

DEAR MR. CLARKE :

The circle of friends who, twelve years ago, were gathered together for social intercourse and weekly reading, through the instrumentality of two ladies, now no longer with us, cannot withhold their united tribute of sympathy to you, in the recent bereavement, which not only you, but they also, have experienced. The removal from a household of a woman as genial and gifted as was Mrs. Clarke is the putting out of the candle which gave light and cheerfulness to all that were in the house; and the depth of your personal loss we will not dare to measure or to gauge. We know, from our own sense of bereavement, how great it must be; and we offer the poor consolation of our sincere sympathy, as we mingle our tears with yours over her, who was one of the originators of our much-esteemed social circle, and who ever continued its most inspiring and interested member.

But, as " friend after friend departs," and the memories of the members gone begin to be as strong in association as the personal presence of the living who remain, there will be none whose name will awaken brighter or more pleasing recollections than that of your wife. Her sweet, gentle spirit, united with that element of heroism which only since her death many of us have fully learned to know was a strong element in her character, will, we trust, help to mould and strengthen that of each one of us, as we move on, in the appointed way, to the end. We may truly say of her, as with you we take leave of her earthly life, —

" Farewell to the dead !
Blest spirit, we will weep no more,
    But lay our selfishness to rest :
The Providence which we adore
    Has ordered all things for the best.
Life's battle fought, the victory won,
To heaven's own joys pass on, pass on."

J. S. FARRAND.	LEWIS ALLEN.
OLIVE M. FARRAND.	JULIA L. ALLEN.
MARY C. FARRAND.	SYLVIA ALLEN.
W. F. RAYNOLDS.	D. BETHUNE DUFFIELD.
MARY H. RAYNOLDS.	MARY B. DUFFIELD.

D. O. FARRAND.
E. T. FARRAND.
H. P. SANGER.
FANNIE H. SANGER.
MARY H. HULBERT.
WM. J. WATERMAN.
ELLA H. WATERMAN.
ALFRED RUSSELL.
ELLEN P. RUSSELL.
PHEBE P. WELLS.

S. ELIZA NOYES.
CLEAVELAND HUNT.
HELEN W. HUNT.
MARY W. LOCKWOOD.
ALBERTINE LOCKWOOD.
SARAH T. E. LOCKWOOD.
J. W. WATERMAN.
WM. JENNISON.
EUNICE A. JENNISON.

(*Extract from a Letter.*)

*   *   *   *   "I have heard from Detroit, that Mrs. Clarke has been released from suffering. As long as I am living on the earth with you, you may always know of one whose heart is most tenderly impressed and deeply moved at the thought of her who has been to you and to all who knew her a very star of joy. So strange and beautiful is the whole impression that your beloved wife has made upon me, that I find it impossible to send you any ordinary expression of my sympathy. I always thought her among those gifted with the *angelic*; and, when I thought of her great struggle with weakness and pain, her spirit seemed to me already on a throne."

(*From another.*)

*   *   *   *   " What a beautiful life hers
has been these years past, radiant with the beauty
of holiness, — the beauty which gladdens the heart of
God and his angels, and makes heaven lovelier than
earth! I do not know that I have ever seen bodily pain
and the weariness of confinement borne with such
sweetness; so that those who only casually saw her,
could scarce think of her otherwise than as one of the
few who have no cause for sadness. So completely, by
the grace of God, did the spirit triumph over the infirm-
ities of the body, that she never made any one feel
that she needed sympathy; but she rather inspired one
with envy of her cheerful, hopeful temperament. Such
was the impression upon me in the little that I saw of
her personally; and so always I have been accustomed
to hear her intimate friends speak of her. And how
wonderfully she seemed to endear herself to all who
came within her sphere! How greatly was it given to
her to honor that Divine Master whose grace made her
what she was! He fashioned her by the discipline of

suffering here, for higher service to which himself has called her. The token that He sent was one by which he often attests the summons to his elect ones, — an arrow, with a point sharpened with love, let into her heart; which, by degrees, so effectually wrought with her, that at the time appointed she must be gone. Her place of service I know is now in the presence of her Lord. Seeing him as he is, with no vail between, she reflects, more radiantly than ever below, his beauty. Her cross is now the crown. She walks in white with the followers of the Lamb."

THE END

www.ingramcontent.com/pod-product-compliance
Lightning Source LLC
Chambersburg PA
CBHW030914260626